# LIVINGSTONE MOUSE

## MOUSE

by Pamela Duncan Edwards
illustrated by Henry Cole

HarperCollinsPublishers

Livingstone Mouse was an explorer.

He spent his days running here and there, investigating this and that.

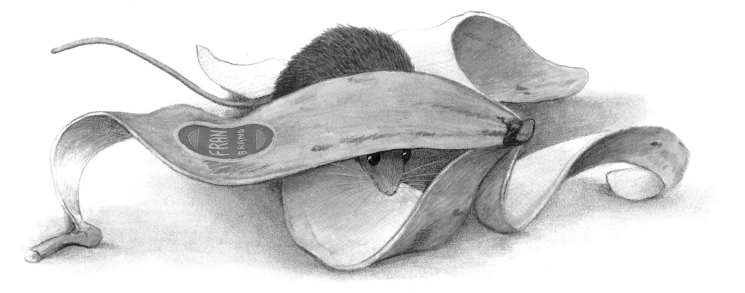

One night, Livingstone's mother said to her little mice, "You've grown too big to live in my small nest. It's time for you to find places to build nests of your own."

"I'd like to build my nest in the greatest place in the world," cried Livingstone. "Mother, where is that?"

"Well," replied his mother, "I have heard that China is very nice."

"That's it," announced Livingstone, kissing his mother good-bye. "I will go to find China."

After a while, Livingstone came to the biggest building he had ever seen.

"It's already divided into nest places," said Livingstone. "That's incredible. This must be China."

"There's lots of room," murmured Livingstone. He sat down to plan his nest.

A loud clicking noise came from next door. Livingstone saw a beetle turning somersaults.

"Excuse me," said Livingstone, "but do you do that often?"

"All the time," replied the beetle. "I'm a click beetle."

Suddenly, an angry voice yelled, "Stay over on your own side."

"Stay over on your own side yourself," yelled a second voice. "I don't know why I live with you—you never stop complaining."

"Excuse me," said Livingstone, "but do they do that often?"

"All the time," replied the beetle. "Cockroaches are so argumentative."

"I had no idea China would be so noisy," cried Livingstone.

"China?" laughed the beetle. "This isn't China. Why don't you try that way?"

10

Livingstone scampered in the direction the beetle had pointed. He found himself in front of a tall, white shape rising majestically into the air. Up one of its slopes ran a rope ladder.

"That's fantastic," said Livingstone. "This must be China."

He ran up the rope ladder and down into the dark interior.

"It's nice and quiet," murmured Livingstone. He sat down to plan his nest.

A nasty, musty, human smell hit Livingstone's nose.

"Ugh!" he gasped. "I had no idea China would smell so bad."

"China?" chittered a camel cricket. "This isn't China. Why don't you try that way?"

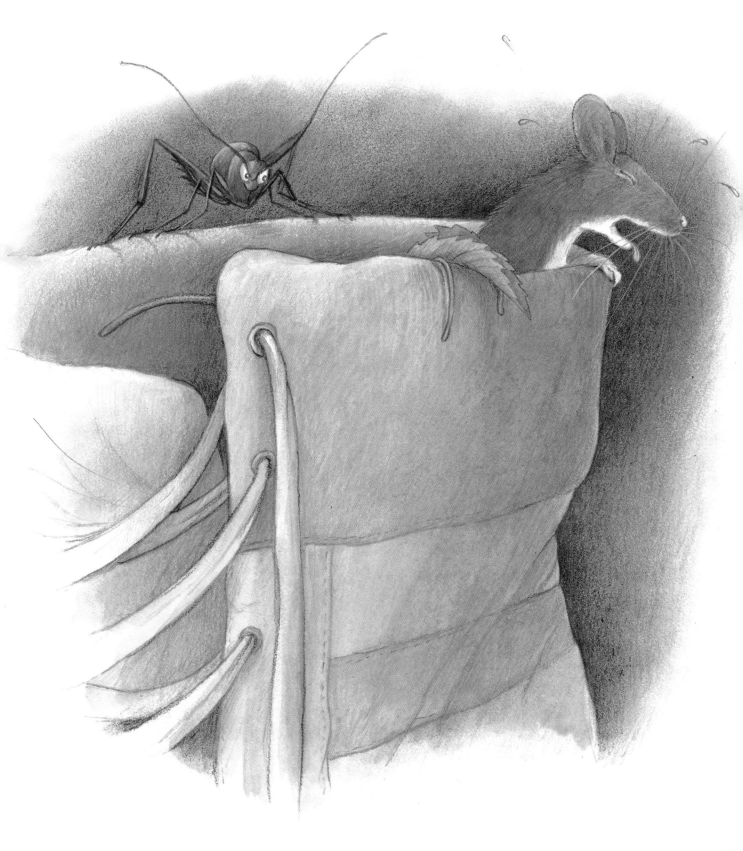

Livingstone ran on, gulping in air to get rid of the nasty smell. He skittered to a halt before a steep slope made out of pieces of thin, woven wood. From the top of the slope, Livingstone could see peculiar objects scattered about a cloth.

"That's wonderful," said Livingstone. "This must be China."

With a leap, he landed on the cloth. "It's quiet, and there's no bad smell," murmured Livingstone. He sat down to plan his nest.

Livingstone noticed a bottle with a big drop of red liquid dripping from its open neck. He took a big mouthful.

"Yeeow!" he howled. "I had no idea food would be so hot in China."

"China?" barked a raccoon, on his way to the trash cans. "This isn't China. Why don't you try that way?"

Livingstone plodded off, his tongue burning. Soon, he came to a square room with an open gate at the entrance. In the middle of the room, a piece of cheese lay on top of a slope.

"That's neat," said Livingstone. "It's quiet, there's no bad smell, and I'm sure that's mouse food. This must be China." He sat down to plan his nest.

Livingstone's mouth began to water at the thought of the cheese. "I'll eat a tiny piece," he thought.

"Run!" someone squealed, so loudly the cheese began to wobble.

"Eek!" screeched Livingstone as the gate clanked down, trapping the end of his tail.

"Dear, dear, dear," fussed the voice. "That was a silly thing to do."

Two large rats heaved at the bottom of the gate.

"You're lucky," said one of the rats, holding up his
tail. "Look what happened to me."

"I had no idea living in China would hurt so much,"
cried Livingstone.

"China?" laughed the other rat. "This isn't China."

"Why don't you try that way?" they said together.

Livingstone scurried across the damp grass, shuddering to think what might have happened to his tail. Eventually, he came to a tall wooden post. Sitting on top of the post was the perfect little house for a mouse.

"That's amazing," said Livingstone. "I love the pointed roof and big picture windows. This must be China."

"It's quiet," murmured Livingstone. "There's no bad smell, no food to sting my tongue, and no mean gate to hurt me." He sat down to plan his nest.

With a loud pop, light flooded the little house, blinding Livingstone. Livingstone wiped tears from his eyes.

"I had no idea nights would be so bright in China," he sighed to a luna moth.

"China?" gulped the moth shyly. "This isn't China. Why don't you try that way?"

Poor Livingstone. He had a headache from too much noise, he felt sick from the bad smell, his tongue smarted, his tail throbbed, his eyes were stinging, and he still hadn't found China. Wearily, he set off again. Then he saw it.

It lay on its side in a
shaft of moonlight, glistening
blues and whites. It had a bridge
to enter by, and a large inner room
with a secret passage leading out on one side.
"Oh!" gasped Livingstone, hardly daring to breathe.
"That is the GREATEST."

A bat glided over Livingstone's head.

"Excuse me," called Livingstone, "could you tell me what that great place is?"

"Oh, that," sniffed the bat. "You don't want to bother with that. That's just some old china."

"Some old China! But I've been looking everywhere for China," cried Livingstone. "This is where I want to build my nest and live happily ever after."

And that's exactly what he did.

*For Geoffrey, who <u>is</u> the greatest.*
*—P.D.E*
*To Fran, explorer and wonderful friend.*
*—H.C.*

Livingstone Mouse
Text copyright © 1996 by Pamela Duncan Edwards
Illustrations copyright © 1996 by Henry Cole
Printed in the U.S.A. All rights reserved.

Library of Congress Cataloging-in-Publication Data
Edwards, Pamela.
    Livingstone Mouse / by Pamela Duncan Edwards ; illustrated by Henry Cole.
        p.       cm.
    Summary: An explorer mouse in search of China discovers that he must be
careful to choose a new home that does not offend his sense of smell, sight,
hearing, taste, or touch.
    ISBN 0-06-025869-1. — ISBN 0-06-025870-5 (lib. bdg.)
    ISBN 0-06-443508-3 (pbk.)
    [1. Mice—Fiction.    2. Dwellings—Fiction.]    I. Cole, Henry, ill.    II. Title.
PZ7.E26365Li   1996                                                    95-19981
[E]—dc20                                                                    CIP
                                                                              AC

Typography by Elynn Cohen
❖
Visit us on the World Wide Web!
http://www.harperchildrens.com